DATE DUE		
FEB 1 0 '95 DEC 0 4 '05		
APR 2 8 '95 APR 1 2 2006		
JUL 21 '95		
AUG 08 '95		
NOV 1 3 '95		
DEC 0 3 1996		
FEB 09 '98		
MAR 0 6 '98		
JUL 02 '99		
APR 1 3 00		
JUL 1 7 01		

HEADQUARTERS:

413 W. Main

Medford, Oregon 97501

GAYLORD M2G

You can be a
Brownie Girl Scout, too!

If you are 6, 7, or 8 years old, or in the 1st, 2nd, or 3rd grade, just ask your parents to look in your local telephone directory under "**Girl Scouts,**" and call for information. You can also ask your parents to call **Girl Scouts of the U.S.A.** at **1-(212) 852-8000** or write to 420 Fifth Avenue, New York, NY 10018-2702 to find out about becoming a Girl Scout in your area.

For Amy and Sarah — J.O'C.

For Austin — L.S.L.

Copyright © 1993 by Girl Scouts of the United States of America. All rights reserved. Published by Grosset & Dunlap, Inc., a member of The Putnam & Grosset Group, New York, in cooperation with Girl Scouts of the United States of America. Published simultaneously in Canada. Printed in the U.S.A.

The "Brownie Smile Song" used by kind permission of Harriet F. Heywood.

Library of Congress Cataloging-in-Publication Data

O'Connor, Jane.
    Make up your mind, Marsha! / by Jane O'Connor ; illustrated by Laurie Struck Long.
      p.   cm. — (Here come the Brownies ; 3)
    Summary: Marsha always has trouble making decisions, but her Brownie friends help her make a difficult choice about whether to go to a sick child's birthday party or to meet a famous ballerina.
    [1. Girl Scouts—Fiction.   2. Decision making—Fiction.]   I. Long, Laurie Struck, ill.   II. Title.   III. Series.
PZ7.0222Mak   1993
[Fic]—dc20   92-45880

ISBN 0-448-40164-9 (pbk)   A B C D E F G H I J

ISBN 0-448-40165-7 (GB)   A B C D E F G H I J

HERE COME THE BROWNIES
A Brownie Girl Scout Book

Make Up Your Mind, Marsha!

By Jane O'Connor
Illustrated by Laurie Struck Long

Grosset & Dunlap • New York
In association with GIRL SCOUTS OF THE U.S.A.

1

"Do your ears hang low?
Do they wobble to and fro?
Can you tie them in a knot?
Can you tie them in a bow?..."

Corrie, Sarah, and Krissy A. were almost halfway through their song.

"Ooh, I'm next!" Marsha whispered nervously to her best friend, Lauren. She nibbled at a fingernail. "I know I'm going to mess up. I should have picked something else to do."

"You say that about *everything*," Lauren whispered. "You'll be fine."

"Can you throw them over your shoulder.
Like a Continental soldier?
Do your ears hang low?"

Corrie, Sarah, and Krissy A. wobbled their droopy puppy ears. It was cute the way they had each pinned a pair of brown socks to a hair band.

Marsha's Brownie Girl Scout troop had come to put on a show for all the kids in the children's wing of the hospital.

Lauren had told knock-knock jokes. Jo Ann juggled three tennis balls. Amy had recited "Mary Had a Little Lamb" in a Donald Duck voice. Krissy S. had played the recorder, although Marsha wasn't sure what song it had been. "Twinkle Twinkle" or maybe "Jingle Bells." Anyway, every Brownie had done something.

"Yes my ears ha-a-a-ng lo-o-o-ow!"

The song was over now. Corrie, Sarah, and Krissy A. took a bow. Their droopy sock ears almost touched the floor.

"I should have picked something funny, too," Marsha thought. "Probably nobody else even likes ballet." But now it was too late to change her mind.

"The music is all set, Mrs. Q." Marsha handed the tape player to her troop leader. Mrs. Q.'s real name was Mrs. Quinones. But all the Brownies called her Mrs. Q.

Marsha picked up her hoop. Then the music began to play. It was the Candy Cane dance from the Nutcracker ballet. As soon as Marsha heard the first notes, she stopped worrying. That was what always happened. Suddenly she just wanted to dance.

Marsha knew the steps to the Candy Cane dance by heart. She'd been watching the older girls at ballet class practice for weeks.

Quickly and lightly Marsha flew through the dance. She had wrapped white tape around her red hoop so it had stripes just

like a candy cane. And the little bells her mother had pinned onto her leotard jingled as she leaped and turned across the floor.

The pace of the music grew faster and faster. So far so good. But now came the hard part. With her candy cane hoop held high, Marsha did two spins. Then she jumped through the hoop.

There! She made it!

Marsha ended with a split. A good split, too. Her legs were hardly bent at all.

Everyone clapped hard. Lauren went thumbs up. Marsha beamed and tried not to breathe heavily. "Never make dancing look like work," her ballet teacher always said.

The sound of applause made Marsha feel so good. As if her heart were growing bigger and bigger.

Marsha was the last Brownie to perform. So now the head nurse of the children's wing stood up. She told the Brownies how much it meant to have them come and visit. Then out came the snacks. Little boxes of juice. And big plates of cookies.

Marsha surveyed the plate of cookies in front of her. Now let's see. There were sugar

cookies. Chocolate chip cookies. Cookies with blobs of jam on them. It sure was hard to make up her mind.

"You were so good," said a little girl standing beside her. She was wearing a pink bathrobe and slippers with bunnies on them.

"Really? Thanks!" said Marsha. "I was pretty nervous before I started."

"You couldn't tell." The little girl popped a chocolate chip cookie in her mouth.

Marsha started to reach for a chocolate chip, too. Then her hand moved over toward a sugar cookie. And from there to one with jam. Gosh, they all looked so good.

"How about picking one today, Marsha," said Lauren. "While we're still young." Lauren gave her a friendly sock in the arm. Then Lauren grabbed a sugar

cookie and went off to talk to one of the
hospital kids. Lauren was not a bit like
Marsha. She talked fast. She ran fast. And
she made her mind up fast. Marsha knew
she sometimes drove Lauren bonkers.

"I bet you take tons of dancing lessons,"
the little girl in the bunny slippers said

as Marsha finally chose a cookie with jam.

"I take ballet once a week." Marsha took a nibble of the cookie. Mmmmmm. It *was* yummy. "Beginning ballet, actually," Marsha told her. "You can't go up on your toes until you are ten or eleven. I'm only eight. Kids my age would really mess up their feet if they tried it." Marsha took another nibble. "I *am* going to be in a real ballet though. The Nutcracker...I'm a mouse." Marsha hoped it did not sound as if she were bragging.

"That's so great!" the little girl said.

Marsha smiled. "I really wanted to be a candy cane. But you have to be ten."

"Last year I went to New York City. My grandma took me to see the Nutcracker."

"Oh, I'm only in the one here in town,"

Marsha explained. "It's not famous or anything. Not like the one you saw. Do you remember who was the Sugar Plum Fairy?"

"Um...Viola Somebody, I think."

"Not Violetta Jamison!"

The little girl nodded. "Yes, I think so."

"Oh, you're so lucky. She's my favorite ballerina. I have a poster of her in my room."

"She was very good," agreed the little girl. "She didn't fall or anything."

Marsha smiled. The little girl still had her baby teeth. She looked like she was the same age as Rosie, Marsha's little sister. It was sad that she was in the hospital. Marsha wondered what was wrong with her. But Mrs. Q. had made it clear. Brownie Girl Scouts were not—repeat *not*—to ask any children what was the matter.

"I'm having an operation tomorrow," the little girl blurted out. She kept her eyes on the plate of cookies. "They have to fix my heart. Something isn't working right. The nurses tell me not to be scared...but I am."

"I know how you feel," Marsha said. "I had an operation when I was six."

"Really?" said the girl. "What was wrong with you?"

"My tummy. I had what they call a hernia. It's sort of like a run in a stocking. Only it's in your muscle. I was very scared, too. I am the biggest baby about shots and stuff." Marsha paused. But the little girl looked interested. So she went on.

"Anyway, I cried so much I got the hiccups. But the operation wasn't so bad. They put this I.V. in your arm. Then— whammo! You are out. The next thing

I knew I woke up. And it was all over."

"My doctor told me the same thing," the little girl said. "But I thought maybe he was just saying that."

"No. It's true. Girl Scout's honor," Marsha said. "And that means it's the absolute truth. I take being a Brownie Girl Scout very seriously." In fact, it was the most important thing to her. Except maybe dancing . . . she never could decide.

It was then that Marsha saw her father. He was standing in the hallway, making frantic waving motions at her.

"Ooh, I have to go. I have Nutcracker practice at 5:00." Marsha bit her lower lip. "I wish I could stay and talk more."

"That's okay. I'm glad you told me about your hyena operation. Or whatever you called it. It makes me feel better."

Marsha nodded. "Well. Good luck tomorrow," was all she could think to say. Then she picked up her pink dance bag and made a dash for the hallway.

2

Marsha's father dropped her off at the town center. Marsha ran up the stairs two at a time. Nutcracker practice was in a different room from her Monday dance class. This room was bigger. And one whole wall was a mirror with a real ballet bar.

In the dressing room, a fourth grader named Lynn waved hello. Lynn was lucky. She was a candy cane.

As always, Lynn had on a red leotard—

the kind that had a flouncy little skirt. It came from a store called "On Your Toes." Marsha had almost $20 saved up. And she was sure—well 99% sure—that she was going to buy a leotard just like Lynn's.

"We'd better hurry. Everybody else is out there," Lynn said. "We don't want Madam to get angry."

Madam was the coach for the Nutcracker. She also danced the part of the Sugar Plum Fairy. Madam was very tall—taller even than Marsha's father. And she always wore lots of dark lipstick. Her father said Madam was "striking" looking. Marsha thought scary was more like it.

Today Madam worked with the mice.

"Remember. You are not little girls anymore. You are r-r-r-rodents." Madam rolled out her words in a dramatic way. "You cannot talk. You squeak. You cannot walk or run. You scurry, scurry, scurry."

Madam demonstrated.

She held her hands up to her chin. She scrinched up her face until it was all pointy and mouse-like. Then off she went on tippy toes. Marsha was amazed. Madam *did* look like a mouse scurrying across the room. It almost seemed as if she had grown a tail!

For the rest of the hour, Marsha and the mice went over the dance. Marsha tried to copy the way Madam scrinched up her face and held her hands. It was fun to be a mouse!

Several times Madam had to remind the girls to do less squeaking and more scurrying. But at the end of the class, Madam said, "Not too bad today." For Madam, that was a big compliment.

Then Madam clapped her hands.

"Before you change your clothes, I have some news," she said. "Two weeks from today, we will have a special guest. Violetta Jamison is coming to watch you practice."

A buzz of excitement went around the room. Violetta Jamison had once been a student of Madam's.

And now Marsha would have a chance to meet Violetta Jamison. In the flesh. This was absolutely, positively the most exciting thing that had ever happened to Marsha!

*   *   *

The next morning the telephone rang.

"Marsha. It's for you," Marsha's brother Terrence shouted to her. "Take three guesses who it is. And the first two don't count."

Terrence always said that when Lauren called. Marsha grabbed the phone.

"Hi," Marsha said. "I can't talk now. Mama is taking me and Rosie shopping. I might get that fancy leotard I told you about."

"Rats!" said Lauren. "It's going to be hot today. I wanted to set up our lemonade stand. Can't you go shopping later?"

"Hold on. I'll ask."

But Mama said later was no good. She had to fix dinner for company. Couldn't Lauren do the lemonade stand in the afternoon instead?

"Sorry, I have a dentist appointment." Lauren sighed. "Too bad. Soon it will be too cold to sell lemonade."

That was true. Besides, selling lemonade was fun. They had a table with a big sign. "All natural ingredients. Nothing artificial added," it said. Lauren's house was right across from some tennis courts. So on a hot day, there were always lots of customers.

Ooooooh! Now Marsha didn't know what to do. Go shopping or sell lemonade. Leotards cost a lot. Maybe she didn't even have enough money yet. If that were so, then selling lemonade would be the right choice. But what if somebody else went to the store and got the last red leotard in Marsha's size? Maybe going shopping was the right choice after all.

"Ooooh, Lauren." Marsha jiggled the phone cord. "I want to do both things." Decisions! Decisions! Marsha hated making decisions.

Finally, Mama came over. "Put down the phone, Marsha," Mama said. "You are coming with me. And that's that."

Marsha shrugged. Okay. Her mind had been made up for her.

At the mall, the first stop was the card shop. Marsha helped her little sister pick out cards for their grandparents' anniversary.

Right next to the anniversary cards was a row of get well cards. That reminded Marsha of the little girl at the hospital—the one in the bunny slippers. She might be having her heart operation this very second!

All of a sudden Marsha felt bad. Here she was carrying on about whether to go shopping or spend time with her best friend. Either one was about a zillion times better than being in the hospital.

Marsha searched through the get well cards. On the front of one was a bunny holding a bunch of balloons. Marsha opened the card. Inside it said, "Hop to it and feel better soon!" It seemed like the perfect card to send.

But what was the little girl's name? Marsha did not have a clue. If only she had asked. Still, maybe Mama could call the hospital later and find out. Marsha fished some money out of her wallet and paid for the card.

After Rosie got new party shoes, they found the store called "On Your Toes."

And there the leotard was! Right on the front rack. A red one in Marsha's size. It was as if the leotard were waiting for Marsha to come in and buy it.

Marsha found a dressing room and tried it on. The leotard did look nice on her. Marsha gazed at the mirror. She loved the tiny straps and the way the skirt swirled around. Then a saleslady tapped on the door.

"These just came in." The saleslady held up a purple leotard with long sleeves and a yellow one that also had a skirt. "I thought you might like to try them on, too."

So Marsha did.

First one. Then the other. Then the red again. Then back to the yellow. And the purple once more. Which one? Which one? Marsha couldn't make up her mind.

Then Rosie started whining. She had to go to the bathroom. Badly. And Marsha could tell Mama was losing patience. Fast.

So Marsha took the leotards back to the saleslady. And they left the store. Except for the get well card, Marsha came home empty-handed.

"I'm hopeless, Mama!" Marsha cried. "I can't make up my mind about anything."

28

"You think things over too much, honey," Mama said. "And you waste a lot of time doing it...that's your problem."

The phone book was in Mama's lap. She was looking up the number of the hospital.

"A lot of times you just have to trust yourself. Go by what you feel. It's called gut instinct." Mama ran her finger down the page. "Ah! Here's the number."

With Mama's help Marsha called the hospital. She found out the girl's name. It was Wendy Levitt. And yes, her operation was over. She was doing fine.

Later, Marsha mailed the card with the bunny on it. She put her name and address on the back of the envelope. And she wrote the whole thing in cursive. That was the grown-up way Mrs. Fujikawa was teaching all the kids in 2-B.

3

The next day, Marsha called the hospital again. But Wendy could not talk on the telephone. Then, on Tuesday after dinner, the phone rang. Terrence picked it up.

"Marsha. It's for you." This time he did not say, "Take three guesses who it is. And the first two don't count."

"Marsha. My name is Sidney Levitt," a man's voice said. "There is somebody here who wants to talk to you very badly."

Marsha knew right away who the somebody was.

"Wendy!" she said. "How are you?"

"Pretty good. It was like you said.. I really didn't feel anything." Wendy's voice sounded kind of froggy and faraway. Wendy thanked Marsha for the card. "I couldn't believe you sent it! That was *so* nice."

Wendy's words made Marsha feel good all over. Being a Brownie meant doing nice things for people. Marsha knew Mrs. Q. would be proud of her. But the nicest part about making somebody else feel good was how good it made her feel. It was like the way Marsha felt when she was dancing. As if her heart were growing bigger and bigger.

Soon Wendy and Marsha said good-bye. Wendy told Marsha she was sending her a birthday party invitation. "I have to have my party here in the hospital. But I hope you can come."

"I'll be there. Girl Scout's honor!" said Marsha. And she meant it.

Sure enough, the party invitation came two days later. Right away Marsha put down the date on the wall calendar in the kitchen.

Now let's see. The 16th fell on a Friday. Marsha started to write in "Marsha goes to Wendy's party" and the time.

That's when she saw it. "Marsha's Brownie meeting 3:00-4:30. Marsha's Nutcracker practice 5:00-6:30."

No one was supposed to skip practice. Madam made that very clear. But it was only one time. And it was for a good cause. For once, Marsha made up her mind. She was going to Wendy's party. It was what a Brownie Girl Scout would do.

That nice, big-hearted feeling came over Marsha again. Maybe this was the "gut instinct" Mama had been talking about.

Marsha went upstairs to do her spelling homework. As always, the poster of Violetta Jamison was the first thing she saw as she entered her room.

Violetta Jamison in the Nutcracker

Then, all of a sudden, it hit her. Next Friday was not just any old practice. It was the day Violetta Jamison was coming.

Now what was Marsha going to do?

4

"Earth to Marsha!" Amy shouted from second base. Marsha was on third. She was rubbing her eyes and holding back a yawn.

All the Brownies were out in the school yard playing kickball. Usually Friday meetings were held in the lunch room. But not today. It was so nice out, nobody had wanted to stay indoors.

It was the last inning of the game. Marsha's side was still a run behind. There were two outs. And nobody was on first.

It was an exciting game. But Marsha was having trouble keeping her mind on it. Maybe that was because she hadn't slept much last night. She kept thinking about Wendy's party. And when she did get to sleep, she had weird dreams.

A big yawn escaped from Marsha as Sarah got ready to kick.

"You can do it, Sarah!" the Brownies on Marsha's side shouted from the bench.

Sarah licked her lips nervously.

Lauren pitched the ball.

Sarah swung back her leg and kicked as hard as she could. The ball went bouncing down the third base line. It looked good.

Sarah started running.

So did Marsha. But she wasn't even halfway home when she saw the ball go whizzing over her head.

Oh no! Someone had thrown the ball home! And the catcher had caught it.

Marsha turned. Better get back to third! But as she started running back, the ball soared over her head again. Now the third baseman was all ready to catch it.

Uh oh! What should she do? It was like a trap. Marsha felt as if her legs were trying to run in two directions. Which way should she go?

In a flash, the third baseman was on her with the ball.

"You're out!" she shouted to Marsha.

The other side started cheering.

"We won! We won!"

Marsha headed toward the bench.

"Sorry, guys. I just didn't know which way to go."

Some of the girls shrugged.

"That's okay. It's no big deal," Sarah said.

Amy was not as forgiving.

"Couldn't you see that Sarah kicked the ball right to third? All you had to do was stay right where you were," Amy said. "Thanks a bunch." Amy was a good player. But she was not always a good loser.

"Oh come on, Amy," Sarah said. "It's not like Marsha got out on purpose."

"And besides, it's just a game," Corrie said. "So don't feel bad, Marsha." Corrie slung an arm around Marsha.

That did it.

Marsha didn't mind Amy yelling so much. But Corrie's kind words put her over the edge.

All at once Marsha started crying. Not just a little. But real boo-hoo crying with big tears that splashed down her cheeks.

"I'm sorry!" she wailed.

Lauren ran over to Marsha. She put an arm around her, too.

"Happy now, Amy?" Lauren snapped.

No. Amy wasn't.

"Oh, Marsha. Me and my big mouth! Please don't cry! I'm sorry."

Marsha just cried harder.

It took Mrs. Q. to calm everybody down. She asked if Marsha was crying over what Amy said. Marsha shook her head no. "Is there something else bothering you?" When

Marsha nodded yes, Mrs. Q. cupped Marsha's face in her hands. "Maybe it's something you'd like to share with us? Because you know we'll try to help." Mrs. Q. looked around the circle of girls. "That is what our Brownie Ring is for. To talk over things that matter to us."

So everybody plopped down in a circle on the grass. Marsha took a deep breath. Then out came the whole story.

"So you see, I promised Wendy that I was coming to the party. And I would like to go. Really. But how can I miss meeting Violetta Jamison? What should I do?"

Everybody in the troop had an opinion.

"Ballet is such a big deal with Marsha. She should go meet the ballerina."

"Right. Wendy will understand."

"I think Marsha should go to the party."

"Me, too. She promised. And a Girl Scout never breaks her promise."

"Oh that's easy for you to say. Marsha was only trying to be nice. She shouldn't have to miss seeing that ballerina…"

Back and forth. Back and forth. It was like watching one of the tennis games at the courts across from Lauren's house.

"Um. Maybe we should take a vote," Marsha suggested. "However it comes out. That's what I'll do."

Mrs. Q. smiled. But she shook her head. "I don't think that would be a very good idea. This is your decision. It's an important decision. And it's up to you to make it. That's part of being a Brownie, too."

Marsha had been afraid Mrs. Q. was

going to say something like that. But deep down inside she knew that Mrs. Q. was right.

As soon as she was home, Marsha got out a sheet of lined paper.

On one side she wrote:

I will go to Wendy's party because:

On the other side she wrote:

I will go see Violetta Jamison because:

She put down every reason she could come up with for both sides.

This is what she had.

I will go to Wendy's party because:

1. It will make Wendy happy.

2. I already said I was coming.

3. I like birthday parties — especially the cake.

I will go see Violetta Jamison because:

1. I want to be a ballerina when I grow up.
2. Violetta Jamison is my favorite ballerina.
3. This may be the only time I ever get to meet her.
4. Madam will be mad if I don't come.
5. It will be exciting and fun.

Marsha read the two lists over. The answer seemed clear.

Okay. Okay. My mind is made up, Marsha told herself. I am calling Wendy now. I will tell her I'm not coming.

Marsha went into her parents' room.

You are picking up the phone right now, she told herself.

Marsha picked up the phone.

You are dialing the hospital right now.

She began to push the buttons. 234-5678.

She got as far as the 4 before she hung up. Marsha made herself try again.

This time she only got to the 3.

I can't make the call! Marsha wailed to herself. She was hopeless, hopeless, hopeless. Marsha threw herself down on her parents' bed. She stared at the wall. Was she always going to be this way?

But then Marsha started remembering something Mama had said. About how she thought stuff over too much. And then it hit her. Maybe she *had* made up her mind. Maybe she couldn't make the call because deep down, she didn't want to.

Making lists didn't mean anything. She had to go by what she felt. Marsha smiled to herself. Her tummy began to unknot.

So this was it—this was what Mama meant by gut instinct!

5

The Friday afternoon Brownie meeting was coming to an end. The girls held hands in a circle and sang the "Brownie Smile Song."

"I've something in my pocket;
It belongs across my face.
And I keep it very close at hand
In a most convenient place.

"I'm sure you couldn't guess it
If you guessed a long, long while.
So I'll take it out and and put it on—
It's a great big Brownie Smile!"

Mrs. Q. waved good-bye to everybody.

"See you next Friday. We're going to start planning for our camp-out."

Marsha got her jacket and the present for Wendy. It was a picture book about a mouse ballerina named Angelina.

In school today she had told her friends about her decision.

"I thought for sure you would meet the ballerina," Jo Ann said as a whole bunch of Brownies left the troop meeting.

"Me, too."

"Me, three." said some other girls.

"Not me." Lauren said. "I knew Marsha would end up at the party. I would have bet all my lemonade money on it."

"You're nice," Corrie said to Marsha. "Not yucky nice. Just nice nice."

Marsha did not know what to say. So she

blew on her fingers and pretended to polish her finger nails on her chest.

Usually lots of mothers came to pick up their Brownies after the meeting. And everybody went their separate ways.

But today a whole bunch of her friends were all leaving together. Lauren and Amy, Corrie, Sarah. The two Krissys. Jo Ann. Even some of the younger kids in the troop.

Marsha walked outside with them.

"Hey, where are all of you guys going?" Marsha asked.

"Oh, nowhere," sang Lauren. "Nowhere special, are we?"

"Oh no!" said Sarah.

"Nooo," said Amy.

A first grader named Lucy who was missing both front teeth started giggling. Lauren shot her a dirty look.

"Well, have fun at the birthday party," Lauren called out. "See you!"

"Yeah. See you," Marsha called back.

In a few minutes her father's car pulled up.

"Hop in, sweetie," he said.

And off Marsha went to the hospital.

*   *   *

"Happy Birthday to you,

Happy Birthday, dear Wendy-y-y-y..."

Marsha sang along with everybody else. With all the balloons and paper streamers, it really did seem like a regular birthday party.

"...Happy Birthday to you!"

Now Wendy took a deep breath and bent down over her cake. The candles lit up her face. She looked so happy! It made Marsha feel happy, too. In two days, Wendy was leaving the hospital for good. That was the first thing she had told Marsha.

"Make a wish! Make a wish!" a kid in a wheelchair shouted.

Wendy closed her eyes and blew.

Whoosh! Out went the candles.

A minute later, Wendy's mom started passing around plates of cake. Wendy made sure Marsha got an extra-big piece—one with a pink rose on it.

Then Wendy opened her presents.

She got the book from Marsha, some board games, and a cool sweatshirt that said "Superstar" in glitter. The last present she opened was from her parents. It was a pair of blue Rollerblade skates.

Wendy's mouth went into a big "O" of surprise. Then she let out a squeal.

Wendy's dad told her she still had to wait until the doctor said it was okay to go skating. But Marsha could tell Wendy didn't mind. Not too much.

After the presents were unwrapped, Marsha took one of the paper cake plates. She made a hat for Wendy with all the pretty bows from her presents. Marsha always liked to do that at parties.

Right away, Wendy put it on.

"Hold it," said Wendy's mom. "I have to get a picture of this."

Wendy put her arm around Marsha.

"I'm so glad you came!" she said. Then they both said "Cheese."

Marsha was glad, too. She had made the right decision. Yes! She was sure of it.

6

Soon Wendy's friends began to leave. But all of a sudden, there was a buzz of excitement outside in the hallway.

The head nurse came hurrying in.

"We have a surprise guest," she said.

Marsha figured Wendy's parents had hired a clown. Or some guy to do magic tricks. But in through the hallway came Lauren, Amy, Corrie—a whole bunch of kids from Marsha's Brownie troop.

What were they doing here??!!

"You are not going to believe who is with us!" Lauren yelled. She grabbed Marsha. Then she waved her arms toward the hallway.

"Ta-da!" Lauren shouted.

A dark-haired lady appeared. She was tiny for a grown-up. Still, there was something BIG and important about her. She was not wearing a lacy tutu, of course. Or a fairy queen crown. But there was no mistake about it.

It was Violetta Jamison!

The head nurse took Violetta Jamison over to meet Wendy and her parents. Then Violetta turned to the rest of the children.

"Now, which one of you girls is Marsha?" she asked.

Marsha raised her hand. Why did she do that? It was not as if she was in school! "Me," she squeaked.

Violetta held out her hand to Marsha. She was every bit as beautiful as she looked in Marsha's poster. Even the way she lifted her head and turned her neck was beautiful. Like a swan. Or a queen.

Marsha took Violetta's hand and managed to do a little bob of a curtsey. She was afraid it came out looking more like she had a cramp in her leg. But it was all she could manage.

"I am so sorry you could not be at the dance practice today. But your friends told me why." Violetta smiled at the Brownies. "And it was for a very good reason."

Her friends! Marsha remembered all the girls trooping off from the meeting.

"You all went to Madam's class?"

"Yup!" said Lauren. She acted like it was not such a big deal. But to Marsha, the idea of the Brownies barging into Madam's class seemed amazing. Almost more amazing than Violetta Jamison being here!

"The girls asked me if I could come again next week. So you could meet me. But unfortunately, I must fly to Paris tonight. I am on my way to the airport now, in fact. Still, I thought it would be nice to make a stop here...and so—voilà!" Violetta spread out her arms. "Here I am!"

"I can't believe this!" Marsha said. Then she said it again. "I have a poster of you in my room. I took down the Little Mermaid to put you up."

Violetta laughed. "*That* is an honor." Her laugh was musical. Like bells.

Violetta spent a few minutes more chatting with Wendy's parents and the nurses. She signed a few autographs, too. But it was clear to Marsha that most of the kids had no idea who she was.

Then it was time for Violetta to go. She motioned to Marsha. "Please. Come walk me to the car."

Somehow Marsha's legs moved. And she followed Violetta down the hall and out into the lobby of the hospital. It felt sort of like she was sleepwalking.

A long shiny black limousine was waiting.

"This is your first year in the Nutcracker, isn't it?" Violetta asked as she opened the door of the car.

Marsha nodded. "I'm one of the mouses." Yipes! She sounded like a four-year-old! "I mean mice."

Violetta smiled. "I remember my first Nutcracker. How excited I was. And how nervous."

"Yeah. Me, too!"

"So I would like to give you something. It will be for good luck." Violetta pulled a velvet ribbon from her bag. "Here. Please take this. Perhaps you can wear it under your mouse mask."

Marsha took the ribbon. It was a beautiful shade of violet. Just like the one Violetta had in her hair.

"Oh, thank you," Marsha breathed. "I will keep it forever."

Violetta slid into the limo.

"I know you will be wonderful in the ballet. Madam has told me what a promising young dancer you are."

Madam said that!

Then Violetta shut the door. She waved from the window. "Good-bye!"

"Good-bye!" Marsha called back.

Then several other voices joined her.

"Bye!"

"Have a good trip!"

Marsha looked up. Her Brownie friends were waving from one of the hospital windows.

61

"Bon voyage!" shouted Lauren.

Marsha smiled and shook her head. That Lauren! What a friend! But, of course, it hadn't been *just* Lauren. Marsha smiled again. A great big Brownie smile. She bet she had the best friends in the whole world.

Marsha watched the limo disappear around a corner. She held the violet ribbon close to her. And—really and truly—she felt as if her heart was growing a whole size bigger.

Girl Scout Ways

Marsha and her Brownie Girl Scout troop had a lot of fun putting on a talent show for the children in the hospital. You and your friends can put on a show, too!

When you organize your show, it's important to make sure that everybody does something different. One person could play a musical instrument. Somebody else might sing a song, tell jokes, or juggle.

- One neat idea for an act is to play shadow charades. Shadow charades are like regular charades except that the "shadow" part makes them special. To set up the "shadow" part you'll need to hang up some sheets in front of the audience. A bright light behind the sheets will create fun shadows for the audience to see.

- When you play shadow charades, you can pretend to be different animals, just like Marsha pretended to be a mouse at Nutcracker practice. You can be a mouse, or an elephant, an alligator, a lion, a monkey, or anything, really. Just think of what that animal looks like and how that animal moves. Then do your best to look and act just like it. Practice beforehand with someone watching from the audience side to make sure your shadow looks like the animal you want to be.

- The audience will have a great time guessing what kind of animal you are pretending to be!